W9-BWU-437

frog

For my dad. I'm sorry I threw your chess pieces out the window.
—D.P.

For Darryl, the best LITTLE brother a BIG brother could ask for.
—M.B.

Text copyright © 2016 by Dev Petty
Jacket art and interior illustrations copyright © 2016 by Mike Boldt

Visit us on the Web! randomhousekids.com

Educators and librarians, for a variety of teaching tools, visit us at RHTeachersLibrarians.com

Library of Congress Cataloging-in-Publication Data
Names: Petty, Dev, author. | Boldt, Mike, illustrator.
Title: I don't want to be big / by Dev Petty ; illustrated by Mike Boldt.
Description: First edition. | New York : Doubleday, [2016] |
Summary: Little Frog does not want to grow up, and he gives his father all sorts of reasons why being small is best.
Identifiers: LCCN 2015030365 |
ISBN 978-1-101-93920-8 (hc) | ISBN 978-1-101-93921-5 (glb) | ISBN 978-1-101-93922-2 (ebook)
Subjects: | CYAC: Growth—Fiction. | Size—Fiction. | Frogs—Fiction.
Classification: LCC PZ7.P448138 Iak 2016 | DDC [E]—dc23

MANUFACTURED IN CHINA
10 9 8 7 6 5 4 3 2 1
First Edition

I DON'T WANT TO BE BIG

written by Dev Petty illustrated by Mike Boldt

DOUBLEDAY BOOKS FOR YOUNG READERS

4
3
2
1
Well...first you're one inch, and then two inches, then three....
When does it stop?
frog

You can't stay small forever.
An ant stays small forever.
So now you want to be an ant?
Not really.

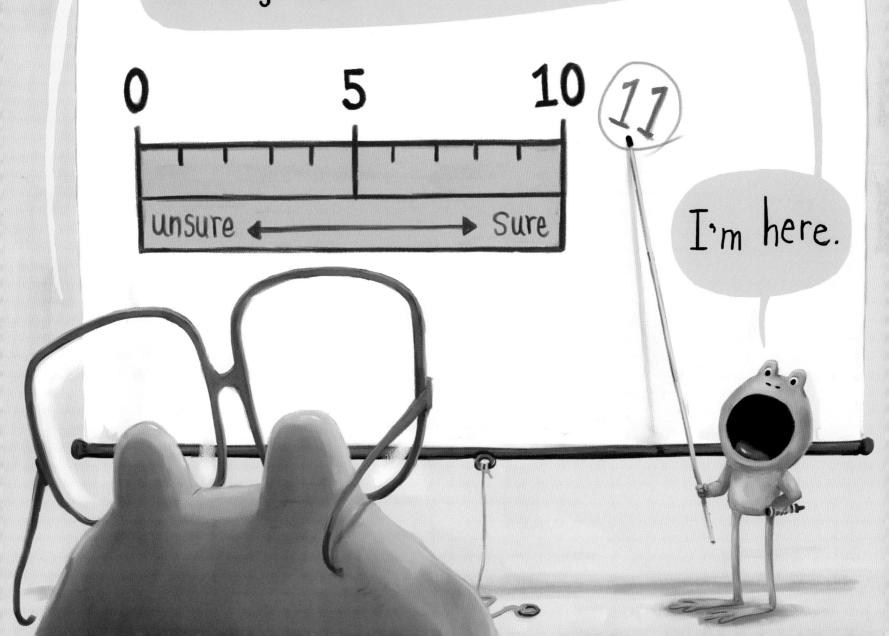

What's the trouble?

I don't want to be big.

Well, Frog, things just have a way of **growing**. And there are good things about growing too.

You're closer to the SUN?

Actually that has its drawbacks.

You get to wear **huge shoes**?

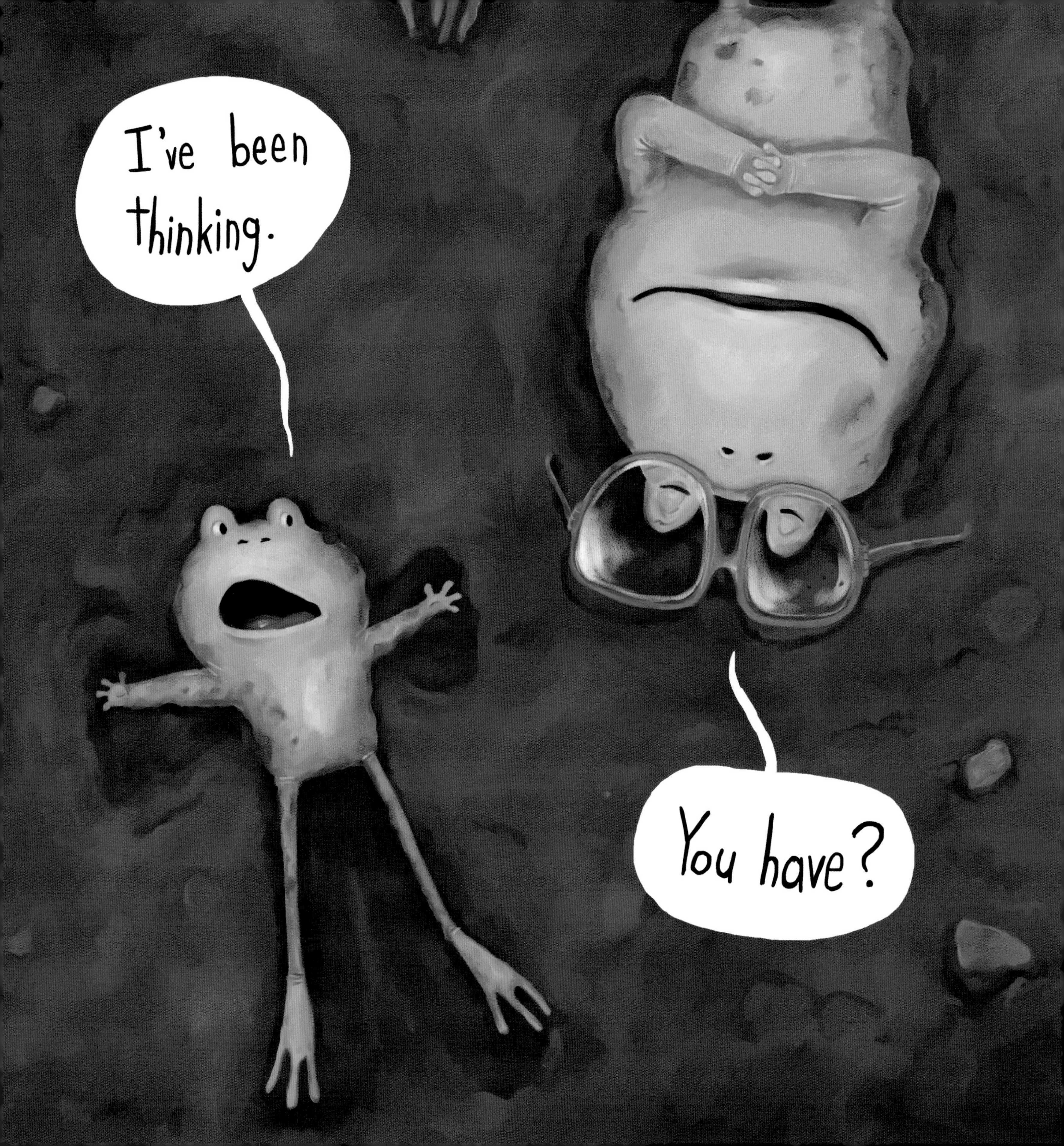
I've been thinking.
You have?

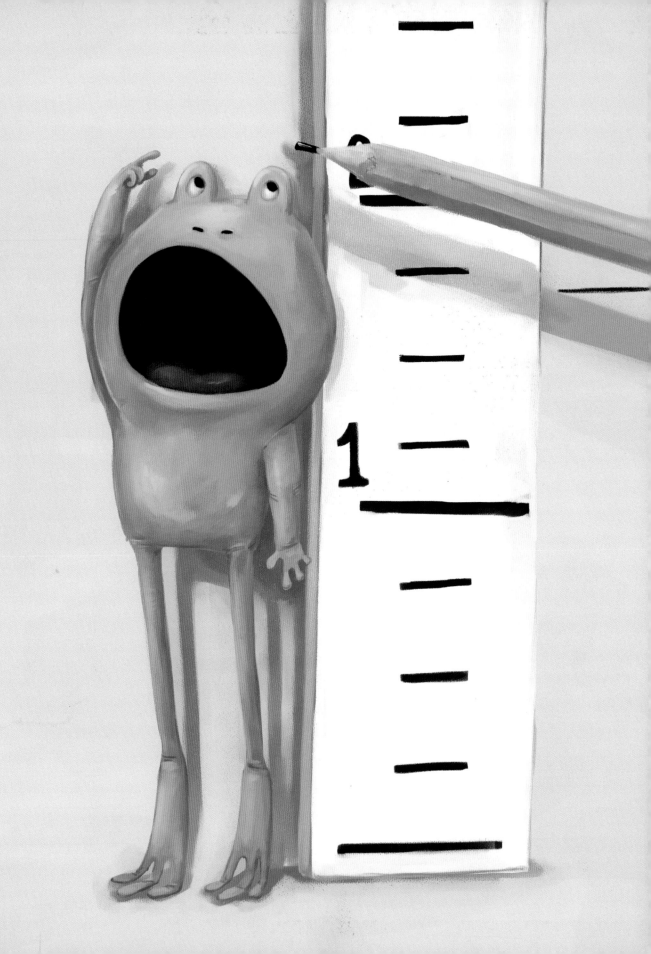